The Half-A-Moon Inn

HARPER & ROW, PUBLISHERS

NEW YORK

Cambridge
Hagerstown
Philadelphia
San Francisco

London
Mexico City
São Paulo
Sydney

1817

The Half-A-Moon Inn

Paul Fleischman

Illustrations by Kathy Jacobi

The Half-a-Moon Inn
Text copyright © 1980 by Paul Fleischman
Illustrations copyright © 1980 by Kathy Jacobi
All rights reserved. No part of this book may be
used or reproduced in any manner whatsoever without
written permission except in the case of brief quotations
embodied in critical articles and reviews. Printed in
the United States of America. For information address
Harper & Row, Publishers, Inc., 10 East 53rd Street,
New York, N.Y. 10022. Published simultaneously in
Canada by Fitzhenry & Whiteside Limited, Toronto.

Library of Congress Cataloging in Publication Data
Fleischman, Paul.
    The Half-a-Moon Inn.

    SUMMARY: A mute boy is held captive by the strange
proprietress of an inn.
    [1. Kidnapping—Fiction.   2. Mutism—Fiction.
3. Physically handicapped—Fiction.   4. Hotels,
motels, etc.—Fiction]   I. Jacobi, Kathy.   II. Title.
PZ7.F599233Hal   [Fic]   79–2010
ISBN 0–06–021917–3
ISBN 0–06–021918–1 lib. bdg.

Also by Paul Fleischman

THE BIRTHDAY TREE

.

The Half-A-Moon Inn

1

Aaron awoke to the sharp cry of sea gulls, suddenly remembered what day it was and burst out of bed as though the sheets were afire. He could hear that his mother was already up, hitching the horse to the wagon. He scrambled into his clothes, scooped up an armload of woolen cloth and shot out the door—for today they'd be traveling to Craftsbury!

"Whoever you are behind all that wool—good morning to you!" called his mother. Aaron smiled and scurried by her, his arms piled high with the wool she'd washed and dyed and spun and woven into cloth. He felt as restless as a chipmunk on the first day of spring, for it was but once every month that they left the seacoast behind them and wound their way through the forest to Craftsbury, where all the world seemed to gather on market day.

There'd be farmers and fortune-tellers, chandlers and capmakers, all shouting their wares at once. The smell of roasting chestnuts would drift through the air, above squealing pigs and bleating lambs and crowds of people swarming about. It was there that Aaron and his mother would sell their cloth, returning home the next morning with oats and lamp oil and more raw wool, to be dyed the colors of the ocean deeps and woven into cloth textured like the sea itself.

"There's breakfast a-waiting for you," called his mother, "if you can stay put in one place so's to eat it." Aaron darted in and out of the one-room house, fit the last load of cloth in the wagon and glanced out at the sea. The waters were still and speckled gold with the sun, and though the early November air was chilly, there wasn't a cloud to be seen in the heavens. A fine day indeed for a journey.

He dashed back inside and sat down to a bowlful of barley gruel. Then he pulled a stub of chalk from his pocket, took up his slate and wrote: "Couldn't we leave now and eat later?" For Aaron had been born unable to speak.

"Well now, I've my own question to ask of you

first, my dove. Don't you come due for a birthday tomorrow?"

Aaron nodded his head.

"And won't you thereby arrive at a full twelve years of age?"

He nodded again.

His mother put down her spoon, and ran her fingers through her long brown hair.

"You see, my dove, I've been thinking." Her voice was hesitant, her eyes scanning him. "And I believe it's come time for me to let you learn to pull your own oars and steer your own rudder, like other boys of your age. And so I want to ask you, Aaron, if you'd be a-willing to do something even more adventuresome than traveling to Craftsbury."

Aaron looked puzzled. "What?" he wrote on his slate.

"I want you to stay here while I'm gone."

A chill darted up his spine.

"Alone?" he wrote.

"Yes, alone."

Aaron gazed at his mother. Never before had he been out of her sight for more than a few hours, much less overnight. With his father lost at sea, there'd been no one but his mother to raise him. And though she'd taught him to read and write as soon as he was able, she'd still feared to let him stray out into the world alone, afraid that he'd stumble into danger without a voice to call for help, or that he'd be mocked for his muteness or even stoned to death as being devil-possessed. Aaron had always been accustomed to having her near, and like the ocean itself, her presence was woven into the background of all of his memories. Yet he knew what she expected of him, and though a nervous dread tugged against him like an outgoing tide, he picked up the chalk, and wrote: "I'll stay."

A smile rose into her eyes. "I'm proud of you, my dove."

But Aaron was too full of apprehensions to feel warmed by her pride. What if something went wrong—if the house caught fire or was struck by lightning or the waves washed in from the sea? Suddenly he thought of changing his mind and going along with her after all, imagining himself up on the wagon where he always sat, sailing grandly through the forest, with the morning air sharp and the birds flitting gaily about the trees—then he awoke from the vision, knowing that it wasn't to be.

His mother finished her barley and rose up from the table. "You'll do fine, my dove," she said to him.

She moved about the room, filling a basket with food for the journey. "I'll put up overnight at The Peacock's Tail, and be home noon tomorrow, just as always. And not one moment later."

She stopped what she was doing and looked into Aaron's face. "There's just one thing you'll have to remember, my dove—and that's never to leave sight of the house. For there's no town to be reached but by traveling inland, where the roads wriggle about the forest like a family of snakes, broad and fine as the king's highway one minute and dwindling down to rabbit runs the next. Always keep close to the sound of the waves, for the woods are full of wolf packs and bears, and a-crawling with brigands like a corpse full of maggots."

A shiver swept through Aaron as he recalled how only last month on the journey to Craftsbury they'd passed Lord Tom himself, the most notorious highwayman of all Bingham Woods. He was raging in a fury, with his huge arms bound with chains and his great red beard flying madly in the wind, having been captured at last and being escorted to prison to be hanged once and for all. Aaron shuddered at the memory of his snarling face, with his one blue eye and his other brown, and Aaron tried to shake off the sight of the man as he got up from the table, picked up his mother's basket of food and accompanied her out to the wagon.

"There's oil in the lamps and food in the cupboard and no need to worry, my dove."

Aaron gazed up the road, following it through the dry, brown fields and into Bingham Woods in the distance. His mother kissed him on the cheek and climbed onto the wagon. Handing the basket of food up to her, Aaron felt lonely and abandoned, longing to be up on the wagon as she was, going where she was going.

"There's only one thing that'll be out of the ordinary," she said. "I'll be a-bringing you back a certain something for your birthday, something befitting such a hardy young man."

Aaron tried to look cheered.

His mother smiled down at him. "Good-bye, Aaron."

He waved good-bye.

"I'm proud of you, lad," said his mother, and she flicked the reins and headed off toward the trees.

2

Long after the wagon had disappeared into the woods, Aaron remained standing where he was, staring off in its direction, following along with his eyes where he imagined it to be. Sea gulls circled and squawked overhead. A breeze blew through his hair, and at last he turned back toward the house and lay down in the grass, gazing out at sea.

. After all, it was only half a day's journey to Craftsbury, he said to himself. She'd be back soon enough—why, tomorrow at noon, and not one moment later. He'd begun to feel better already. And there'd be a birthday present coming home with her as well! He broke into a smile, feverishly wondering what it might be. His mind was aflutter with visions as he lay there, listening to the gulls and feeling the sea breeze on his face, when he suddenly realized he was all on his own—and free to do whatever he wished. He felt airy and light and bursting with energy, and he began rolling in the grass, dizzily, joyfully, squealing with laughter inside. Staying home all alone would be grand!

He picked himself up and scampered down to the beach. Immediately he remembered what his mother had told him, and he looked back at the house, perched just beyond the grasp of the tides. His father had loved the solitude of the sea, and he'd cleared the road that led down from the forest by himself and built a house at its end. Small and white with a thick thatched roof, it was stuck out on a point jutting into the ocean, where there were no other houses about, and under its gaze Aaron gleefully passed the morning.

He skipped stone after stone on the water. He scrambled about the rocks like a crab. He imagined himself a mighty orator, addressing the waters in a thundering bass, commanding the very ocean as though he were its captain.

"Break now, waves, and split your ribs on the rocks! Let the spray fly up, let the waters foam! Fishes—swim! Snails—crawl! Sea gulls—dive for

8

your dinners in the sea!" He could hear himself clearly inside his head, shouting out his orders in a fine, deep voice, trilling his *r*'s magnificently, casting his words out over the water, all the way to the horizon.

When he grew hungry, Aaron walked back to the house and kindled a fire in the stove. He cooked himself a bowl of buckwheat groats and returned once again to the beach, peering into tide pools and scanning the horizon, imagining himself a sailing man like his father. All afternoon he busied himself, and when the sun at last edged back behind the trees and shadows spread onto the beach, Aaron reluctantly walked back home, hungry and tired and with his pockets full of shells.

It was growing dark in the house, and he lit one of the lamps, built a fire in the stove and placed a pot of peas on to boil. Night was coming on and the breeze picking up, with a few ragged clouds blowing in from the sea. He listened to the wind as it rushed over the house, rattling the windows and fluttering the flame in the lamp, and felt a chill pass through him.

Swiftly the light left the sky. Outside, the waves crashed blindly against the rocks in the blackness, and suddenly the house seemed empty and abandoned, as though its last owners had long since left it to the spiders and swallows. Aaron gazed slowly about the room, at the spinning wheel, at the clock his father had brought back from his travels, at the massive loom, still and silent in the corner. The house felt as lifeless as a tomb, and he longed to hear the sound of his mother spinning, or of her softly singing while she wove.

Aaron pulled his chair up next to the stove, his eyes alert and his ears tensed to every sound in the wind, suddenly believing himself to hear footsteps approaching, then distant thunder, then the clatter of horses' hooves. He stared at the wall across the room, and seemed to see it almost imperceptibly bulge and sink, like skin over a heart. The wind roared over the house in a rage when he rose to fetch himself a bowl of porridge, and he ate as quickly and quietly as he could, trying to keep from looking out the windows, for fear of what he might see.

When he was through with his dinner Aaron sat for a while, letting the fire burn down. Then he latched the door, blew out the lamp and climbed quickly into bed. He lay there listening to the wind whistling by on the other side of the wall, glanced out the window across the room and beheld an entire armada of clouds, silently riding the wind in from the sea. He watched them passing before the stars, as stealthily as spies, gazed at them endlessly migrating across the sky and slowly fell into sleep.

When he awoke in the morning, Aaron sensed a chill in the air. He looked out the window, dashed out of bed and threw open the door in disbelief. Snow was falling thickly out of the sky.

He darted back across the room and jumped into his clothes, shivering in the cold and with his teeth chattering at a gallop. Never had he known the first snow of the winter to arrive so early. Usually it didn't come until Christmas—and then only a dusting of snowflakes at that. But this!

Aaron squeezed into his boots and ventured outside, to find his feet sinking into a full half foot of snow. The fields were covered completely, and the woods in the distance were white. It must have been snowing all night.

He looked about in amazement, walked back inside and lit a fire in the stove. What would become of his mother? A half foot of snow wouldn't hold up the wagon, and she'd said she'd return home by noon, just as always. He peered out the window at the road, but could barely make it out under the snow. Surely she wouldn't leave him here longer than she'd promised—not on his birthday.

Aaron shed his coat and his cap and sat down by

the stove. The wind had died down during the night and there wasn't a sound to be heard from outside save the movement of the waters and the brush of snow against the windows. Hour after hour he waited, keeping watch on the road that led from the forest, gazing at the snow drifting down.

He glanced at the clock. The hands said noon. He walked outside and stood peering up the road, but his mother was nowhere in sight.

He tramped back inside and put more wood on the fire. Where could she be? He heated the porridge he'd cooked the night before, but found he wasn't hungry. He decided to whittle a piece of driftwood, but couldn't stop his eyes from wandering to the window, and he put his knife away.

All afternoon he waited, keeping his eyes away from the clock, staring out the window in expectation. Snow continued falling without end, and slowly the light departed from the sky. Aaron tried to keep his thoughts at bay by busying himself with making a pot of potato soup—his mother's favorite kind. He lit all the lamps, built up the fire blazing hot and set the table for two, with the wooden spoons she'd carved herself and her treasured blue-enameled bowls—as if to lure her in out of the darkness.

He decided not to eat until she arrived. He waited an hour. Two hours.

Surely she'd just gotten a late start this morning, or been merely slowed down by the snow. Why, she was bound to show up, and any minute at that.

Another hour passed. At last Aaron couldn't wait any longer, and he ate his dinner alone. He was ready to fall asleep in his chair but he refused to turn in, forcing himself to stay awake. He cocked his ear to the sound of the snow scratching against the windows like a cat, desperate to make of it horses' hooves and the sound of wheels turning.

Finally he could keep his eyes open no longer. He rose from his chair, made certain the door was shut tight, but left it unlatched. He placed a lamp before the window that faced the road, turned it down low and looked out one more time. Then he climbed into bed, and fell asleep waiting for the sound of a wagon.

At dawn he awoke with a start, sprang out of the sheets and stopped in his tracks. His mother's bed was still empty.

What could have happened? He'd been certain she'd be there in the morning, sure she'd have arrived during the night, creeping inside quiet as a mouse, careful not to wake him.

Aaron ran to the window and looked out. He peered through the snow still falling from the sky, but nowhere was his mother to be seen.

He glanced around the room, and noticed her thick winter coat on the rack by the door—she hadn't thought to take it along. Suddenly, everything she'd warned him of leaped into Aaron's mind, and he was struck with the fear that she wasn't just late—but that something had happened to her.

Could she have lost her way in the woods, with the roads covered with snow? Had the wagon become mired in a drift? Had she been attacked by a wolf pack, or a bear, or been fallen upon by thieves? Was she lost in the snow somewhere this very moment, shivering in the cold, calling for help?

He remembered what she'd said about leaving sight of the house. But surely she hadn't meant for him to stay home at a time like this. Perhaps she was stranded just a mile from home. And if she were still close to Craftsbury—why, he'd ridden those roads every month of his life. He'd find his way through the forest, sure as an owl. After all, his birthday had passed, he was a full twelve years old—and she'd expect him to act it.

He rushed about the house, found a large burlap sack and filled it with food, enough for himself and his mother for several days. He packed his flint, a pot and a spoon, paper, pen and ink. He put on his scarf and his mittens and brought his mother's along, drew on his plaid wool coat and put her own coat on over it, so she'd have it to wear. He stood in the center of the room, glancing nervously about, looking for anything he might have forgotten. Then he walked to the door, and set out to find her.

3

Up the road Aaron marched, with the snow knee-deep on the ground now and still blowing down from the clouds. His feet felt pinched, for he'd outgrown his boots, and the wind numbed his face till it felt like stone. The sound of the sea faded as he tramped along, the sack slung over his shoulder and his mother's coat dragging in the snow.

At last he arrived at the edge of the forest, passed in among the trees and came to a fork in the road. He bore to the right, just as he remembered his mother doing, and sharpened his eyes for any sign of her. Deeper into the woods he walked, the trees leafless and bare and their tops swaying in the wind. Soon the road divided again, and again he bore right. Hour after hour he trudged through the snow, treading his way through the maze of the woods, stopping to eat when his stomach grew empty and moving on through the forest again.

It was late afternoon when Aaron came to another fork in the road and stopped, looking about in bewilderment. He struggled to find something familiar to seize on, but nothing he saw set his memory in motion. He stared at the sky, at the trees and the road, and realized that riding along in the wagon was different from guiding it. He turned and looked about for the ocean, but it was nowhere in sight. He climbed up a tree, and saw only more trees, stretching endlessly to the horizon in every direction.

He cursed his memory but vowed not to turn back. He took note of the wind and the path of the sun—and suddenly felt certain that he ought to bear left, and struck out up the road.

The wind swept angrily out of the sky, driving the snow in his face and moaning two-voiced through the trees. Onward he trudged, the road twisting like an eel and growing ever more narrow, while the branches gesticulated wildly in the wind, as if desperately struggling to be understood.

Snow streamed down, filling in the trail of footprints behind him, and slowly the light began to fade. Soon the road tapered down to a trickle so that

Aaron had to search for it anew every few steps. Still he pushed ahead, tired and hungry, groping for the trail among the trees.

At last he stopped—and could go no farther. He looked all about him, but there was nothing resembling a path to be seen. At once he was certain of just what he'd feared—that the road no longer lay under his feet. Somewhere it had escaped him under the snow; he'd simply been dodging between trees for the last hour. And now he was lost, with night coming on.

Quick as a squirrel, Aaron climbed up a tree and snapped off a few dead, dry branches and kindled a fire. He melted snow in his pot and poured in some barley, rolled a rotten log from its place and stretched out on the dry ground beneath it.

The snow had stopped falling and the wind had died down, and he lay there staring into the flames, wondering what he would do in the morning. He could always head into the rising sun and eventually get back to the sea. But he made up his mind to find his way into Craftsbury and to get help for his mother there if he'd not found her first.

Night had arrived, and he devoured the barley and drank the water he'd cooked it in. Then he warmed himself by the fire, wrapped himself up in the two winter coats and lay back on the ground.

19

He listened for the sound of wolves approaching, or robbers returning to their lair, but heard nothing but the soft rustle of branches. Slowly the clouds began to break up, revealing behind them the endless heavens, and the moon in the west. The night air was chill and edged with ice, and Aaron lay there in the stillness, watching the stars go sleep-walking across the sky, before he slipped at last into sleep.

All the next day Aaron wandered through the woods, guiding his aching feet among boulders and brambles, searching for a road that would take him to Craftsbury. From sunrise to dusk he trudged through the snow, without a sign of his mother, or anyone else. At night he built a fire and cooked himself dinner and slept out under the shivering stars.

On the third day of his journey he tramped until noon, and slowly became aware of a strange scent in the air. He sat himself down on a log to rest, sniffed at the breeze—then jumped to his feet.

Of course, it was smoke! Smoke from a fire—there had to be someone nearby.

He followed the smell as best he could, and suddenly spotted a passage through the trees. Finally he'd found his way to a road—perhaps he could reach Craftsbury this very day!

He charged through the snow and struck out up the road, the smell of smoke growing stronger with every step. All of a sudden the scent of food filled the air, Aaron rounded a bend—and there, up ahead, with two wheels sunk in the snow, stood a wagon full of rags and a man cooking beside it.

At last he'd found help! The man was squatting, stirring a pot over a fire, with his back turned to Aaron. Burly and dressed as raggedly as a scarecrow, he appeared to be a ragman who'd become stuck in the snow. Aaron was filled with hunger by the smell of the food, and was eagerly making his way up the road, when he stepped on a twig. The man's horse raised its ears, the ragman whirled about and aimed a pistol straight at Aaron's heart.

"Keep where you be, me suckling cutthroat!" The ragman's eyes bulged wide and afraid, moving quickly over Aaron and scanning the trees behind him.

"And tell the rest of your band of marauders that I'll be glad to give the lot of 'em free passage to hades—if they care to come get it!"

Aaron stood perfectly still, his heart pounding madly, while the ragman nervously eyed the trees again, his gun following along with his glance. The two of them faced each other in silence for several moments, the ragman's ears alert and his eyes darting about. Then he looked once again at Aaron's frightened appearance and at last seemed satisfied that the boy was harmless and alone and cautiously lowered his pistol.

"Can't a man be too careful, lad—not in the woods. More thieves than trees in a place like this. A fearsome bunch of scoundrels, they are, and generous with their shot. Command the very bees to stand and deliver their honey."

He ran his eyes over the forest once again. "But what might such a one as you be doing here, me boy?"

Aaron pulled out the pen and ink from his sack, took off his mittens and rubbed his hands. On a white sheet of paper he wrote: "Have you seen my mother, Mrs. Amelia Patrick, the weaver, of Hifton Head? I can't speak."

He stepped forward and handed the note to the ragman, who opened his eyes in utter amazement.

"Bless me bats," he muttered. "I can see I judged you wrong, me lad, and that you been well brought up to read and write, and not such a boy as would steal." He tucked his pistol away with an air of apology and stared at the paper again.

"Aye, it's a fine hand you've got, lad, it is indeed. But tell me now—what does it say?"

22

Aaron looked back at the ragman in disbelief. Having spent his life with his mother and rarely having left the house, Aaron had always assumed that everyone was able to read and write. How could he explain himself if the man couldn't read?

Quickly he took another sheet of paper from his sack, sketched a portrait of his mother as best he could, and next to it the cathedral in Craftsbury. The ragman watched with the greatest of interest as he drew. Aaron handed him the paper and looked into his eyes, hoping for a spark of recognition.

"Aye, lad, you've got talent," said the ragman, gazing down at the drawing. He shook his head admiringly, glanced again at the note, and handed them both back to Aaron.

"Handy with a quill, you are, that's easy to see. And just as quiet and polite as you please—aye, I can see you're a boy that's been raised up right, and taught to behave proper before his elders."

Quiet? Polite? The man refused to understand that he was unable to speak!

"And now forgive me own manners for waiting to ask—but are you hungry, me lad?"

Aaron forgot his troubles for the moment and nodded his head.

"Well then!" The ragman gave the pot another stir, filled up two wooden bowls with stew, and the two of them sat by the fire and ate.

"Glad for the company, boy, I don't mind telling you. Been marooned here since morning. The ditch over there was filled up with snow, looked just like the road—till we sunk into it clear to the axle."

Aaron looked at the wagon, leaning down off the road and into the snow.

"Can't seem to get free, between the horse and meself. But maybe you wouldn't mind giving us a hand—and coming along for the ride if you be going our way."

Aaron's ears perked up. Even if he couldn't be sure they were heading toward Craftsbury, anything would be faster than wandering on foot—and they were bound to strike a town soon enough where he could straighten his bearings. Aaron looked up at the ragman and nodded his head, gulped down his food and hopped to his feet.

"Well then!" bellowed the ragman, wiping his mouth with his arm. "Climb up on the wagon then, and take up the whip—and put it to use when I give out a yell."

Aaron scrambled onto the wagon. He watched as the ragman plodded around to its sunken side, took hold between the wheels and shouted out, "Now!" A mighty groan came from the ragman, and suddenly Aaron felt the whole right side of the wagon swing up in the air. Frantically he snapped the whip, the horse burst forward, the wagon creaked—and at last it jerked ahead onto the road.

"Well done, me boy!" the ragman called, as he loaded his things into the wagon. "Well done, indeed, and me thanks to you, lad. Now it's homeward to Williford, if that be agreeable to you."

Aaron had never heard of the place, but he nodded his head just the same.

"And with company besides—all the better, me boy!" The ragman took hold of the reins, gave them a shake—and they were off down the road.

4

All afternoon they drove through the woods. Occasionally they crossed another road along the way, but never once did they come to a house or a town. Aaron nervously wondered just where on the face of the earth he was, and thought of getting off at the next road they came to. But it might take him days before he met another person, someone who could point him to Craftsbury. He'd do better to stay with the ragman.

When it grew too dim to see, they stopped for the night, and set off once again in the morning. The snow had melted away in patches, and they plied the road more easily now, the miles piling up behind them. Slowly the trees became fewer and fewer, and suddenly they were out of the forest entirely and rolling along among open meadows. Aaron looked about him in search of a landmark, but the land was new to his eyes.

After several hours the trees gradually closed in upon the road, the light grew dim and they were in among woods once again. Still they'd passed no other traveler, come to no other town—and Aaron began to grow worried. The trees seemed to be different from those he'd first wandered through. Odd-sounding bird calls, such as he'd never before heard on the journey to Craftsbury, rang out through the woods. The very clouds in the sky looked foreign and strange, and an uneasy feeling crept over him.

Night came on, but the ragman kept driving, finding his way by the light of the moon.

"Ought to make home before morning," he spoke up cheerfully. "And you're welcome to stay, me boy, welcome indeed."

Aaron was untouched by the ragman's good spirits, wondering whether his mother had ever made her way home, or whether the blood in her veins had already chilled to ice—when all of a sudden he glimpsed a light up ahead.

He jumped to his feet and nearly fell out of the wagon. Tugging anxiously at the ragman's arm, he pointed up the road.

"Aye, lad, it's an inn," said the ragman, and all at once it came into sight, a ramshackle, three-story house, lit up bone-white in the moonlight. Suddenly the idea of traveling another mile without knowing where he was seemed unbearable to Aaron. He had to get off while there was a chance—and surely an innkeeper could direct him to Craftsbury.

He motioned frantically to stop when they drew up to the inn, and the ragman tugged at the reins, bringing the wagon to a halt.

"Got the urge to sleep in a proper bed, have you, lad?"

Aaron nodded his head, gathered up his belongings and climbed down to the ground. Then he lifted his cap in thanks to the ragman.

"Never seen such a quiet boy before. But I'm grateful for the company, lad—grateful indeed." And he shook on the reins and was off down the road.

Aaron listened to the wagon fading into the night, then turned toward the inn. Several horses stood hitched out in front, and high up in a window shone a light. A peeling sign by the door read: THE HALF-A-MOON INN. MISS GRACKLE, PROPRIETOR, with a milk-white moon painted in the corner.

Cautiously Aaron walked onto the porch, put down his sack and knocked at the door.

Instantly the light drew in from the window.

There came a tremendous clumping of feet down a stairway, the door jerked open and there, with an oil lamp hoisted over her head, stood a bear-sized woman wrapped in shawls like a mummy.

"Inside, and out of the shivery air with you! Quick, boy!" She yanked Aaron in by the wrist and slammed the door shut. He found himself standing in a room cluttered with tables and benches, felt an unexpected chill in the air and realized it was no warmer inside than out.

"State your business, me little dormouse." Her teeth chattered furiously, her words making clouds in the air. "If it's Miss Grackle you come looking for—well then, you've found her."

Aaron pulled out the note he'd shown the ragman and handed it to her. Miss Grackle held it before her face and squinted her eyes at it upside down, then right side up, then upside down again.

"Well now, that *is* interesting. Thank you, boy." She crumpled it up and tucked it into her huge apron pocket. "Now what do you want with me?"

Aaron looked up at her blankly, unsure what to do.

"Well, what are you doing here all by yourself, and in a coat trailing behind you like the robe of a king? Are you lost, boy?"

Aaron excitedly nodded his head, and suddenly Miss Grackle's eyes lit up.

"Well now," she muttered, "you come to the right place, lad—that you have indeed." She circled about him like a vulture, sizing him up.

"Only answer me this—and mind you keep to the truth." She bent down before him and shone the lamp in his face. "Be you an honest lad?" she whispered.

Aaron nodded his head.

"And can you kindle a fire, boy, and raise up the flames till they crack like whips?"

Aaron nodded again.

"Well now!" Miss Grackle hauled him up a flight of stairs and marched him into a bedroom. She disappeared for a moment, then returned with a mountain of wood in her arms, which she let fall to the floor with a crash.

"Don't mind the callers—they're sound asleep up above us. Just conjure up a blaze, me chipmunk, and I'll consider it the price of a bed for you."

Aaron put down his sack, got down on his knees, and carefully arranged the wood in the grate.

"I'd build it meself, mind you, but for all the bending over, with me back so delicate."

Aaron struck a spark from the flint and watched as the flames sprang up quickly, snapping like flags in the wind.

"Aye, you've got the knack of it, boy, that's sure."

She shook with the chills and thrust her out-
stretched hands nearly into the blaze itself. "And
how is it that such a talented child should be out
wandering the woods all alone?"

Full of hope, Aaron handed her the drawing of his
mother. Miss Grackle gazed at it sweetly a moment,
then thrust it into her pocket.

"Well now, that's nice of you, boy. I'm grateful to
have that." Suddenly her smile vanished. "Now, tell
me how you got here!"

Aaron was at a loss at what to do. She took out his
note and puzzled over it some more.

"Me reading's rusted up, boy—can't find time to
keep in practice the way I'd like. Be a good lad now
and recite it to me."

Aaron shook his head.

"Read it out, I say!"

He shook his head again.

"Disobedient, are you?"

He shook his head.

"Didn't you never learn to use your tongue, boy?"

Aaron paused, and shook his head.

Suddenly she stooped down and peered into his
face. "What are you telling me, lad—that you be
mute-born?"

Aaron nodded.

Instantly her eyes opened wide as an owl's. "Well

now, you turn up right handy, me little inchworm. But tell me, where is it you've wandered from—ah, but you can't tell me that, can you? Oh, but you will, boy, and right soon at that."

She tramped downstairs and brought him up a bowl of cold soup with dumplings. "Eat, boy, till the bowl shines clean, and then shake off your clothes and into the bed with you."

Aaron was hungry and gladly gulped down the soup. When he was through, Miss Grackle swept out of the room with his dishes, and Aaron undressed by the fire and climbed under the covers.

Surely Miss Grackle could point him to Craftsbury, if he could only make her understand. Perhaps one of the guests was even heading there tomorrow! He'd go straight to Mr. Bumby, the miller, when he got there. *He* would help him find her.

Aaron gazed at the fire as it slowly burned down, and in the midst of imagining himself home with his mother, he fell into dreaming.

5

"Rise up, boy—up sharp and to work with you!"
Miss Grackle bustled across the room in the dawn
light, whacked Aaron's legs with a willow switch
and shook him till his teeth rattled.

"Hop to the hearths now, quick, and raise the
flames up tall. Let me see 'em hiss like snakes and
snap their jaws like wolves!" She clutched a shawl
around her shoulders and glared down at him, her
teeth chattering wildly with the cold. "Quick,
boy—or are you deaf as well!"

Aaron rubbed his legs and squinted up at her. He'd
get up sure enough, but not to be nursing fires all
morning. He had to get to Craftsbury—and in a
galloping hurry. He heard footsteps creaking on the

floor above him—the guests were awakening. Surely *one* of them would be heading in the right direction and would offer to take him along.

Miss Grackle reined in her voice to a whisper. "You were dreaming of home last night, weren't you, boy? Sitting about the table, you were, just you and your mother with her long brown hair, color of molasses, sipping soup out of those pretty blue bowls."

Aaron stared up at her in disbelief. It was just as she said.

"Aye, I peeked into your dreams, I did, and inspected 'em close. Oh, you were dreaming of speaking, you were, just laughing and shouting and chattering on like a chipmunk. And while I was watching you, I caught me a glimpse out one of your windows—and what do I see but gulls sailing through the air and blue water clear to the horizon. Aye, lad, and no doubt about it—'twas the sea."

She bore down on Aaron like a bird of prey. "And the sea's practically 'round the other side of the globe from here, boy—that far and then some! Oh, you come a long way from home, me cricket—and *too* long a way to be found again! Why, you'd just as likely catch a June bug in December as find your dear mother sniffing around here after you, *if* she ain't clicking her heels to be rid of you."

She smiled down at Aaron like a jack-o'-lantern. "But I'll be generous with you, boy, more than it pays me, and give you a fine roof over your head and your meals as well, all for the price of your minding the fires and doing your chores. Now what's your name, boy?"

Aaron wouldn't have told her even if he were able, and he shook his head.

"Well, you'll come running to 'Sam' from now on, same as the last one. Makes it easy on me memory that way. Now into your clothes, Sam—and to the grates with you!"

Miss Grackle rushed out of the room and Aaron scampered over to the fireplace and climbed into his clothes. Why was it that she couldn't light the fires herself? She'd said it was her back, but she looked strong enough to him to fire up a volcano. Either way, he had more important things to do than to stay on here as an errand boy—and Miss Grackle would find that out in a hurry. Why, he'd be up and out the door quick as a cat—and let her try and catch him!

All of a sudden he stopped and stared. His two winter coats were gone, and so was his sack. He glanced about the room for them—and saw that his stockings were missing, and his boots as well. He clearly remembered taking them off the night before and setting them by the fire. He searched for them everywhere, hopping from one foot to the other on the icy floor, but they seemed to have vanished completely.

Down the stairs he scurried, flushed with anger. He hunted up Miss Grackle, tugged on her arm and pointed to his bare feet.

"Misplaced your boots, did you?" She tied on her apron, with its pocket as big as a flour sack. "Well then, let it be an inspiration to you to keep the floor as warm as griddles. Now give us a blaze, boy, and be quick about it!"

Misplaced, indeed! They might be tight on his feet, but how would he escape through the snow without them?

"And when the flames are climbing the chimney like ivy you can set your fingers to these," she said, and thrust a basket of vegetables into his arms. Aaron wanted to heave it back at her and make a dash for the door—but he remembered his feet. He needed time to think. He decided to do as she said, building a fire and peeling potatoes for the evening's soup, all the while searching for his boots out the corner of his eye.

Suddenly he heard a clumping of feet down the stairs. The callers, of course! Surely one of them would rescue him from Miss Grackle, and mounted on a horse he could get by without boots. He burst up from his bench and made a run for the stairs, but Miss Grackle got there before him and lashed at his feet with her willow switch.

"Back to your work, boy—quick now!" She chased him hopping back to his seat, his feet stinging as though they'd been stuck into a beehive.

"Didn't your mother ever teach you to obey? Aye, I can see I'm going to have to put some manners in you meself, and teach you to be grateful for me hospitality." She whipped the switch across his toes one more time, and returned to warming herself by the fire.

One by one the callers descended the stairs, yawning and grumbling and still groggy with sleep. There were a half dozen of them, all men, and a rough and ragged lot at that. Quickly, Miss Grackle warmed up some gruel and set Aaron to serving it to the guests, keeping a sharp eye over him all the while. The food smelled awful to Aaron, and he watched in amazement as the guests ate it up briskly. But before the first one to finish had a chance to step out the door, Miss Grackle placed herself in the doorway and cleared her throat conspicuously.

"Much as I hate to offend your innocent hearts," she began, " 'twould weigh down me conscience if I

weren't to warn you before you set out that there's been a right lot of *thieves* about lately."

One man's hand reached instantly for his breast pocket, another man's darted to his cap.

"Thick as rats in a cellar, they are, and pleased to pick you clean as a coat stand. 'Twould be worse than sending a baby into a bear's den not to tell you so, and a burden on me soul as well. So take heed in the woods, me worthy gentlemen, and keep your eyes open. And godspeed to you."

One by one they finished their breakfasts and filed past her. When the last one had mounted his horse and set off, she turned to Aaron and burst out laughing.

"Oh, but it's nice to have me a boy such as you, one who'll keep me secrets locked up tight as artichokes." Aaron watched as she pulled two money pouches out of her great apron pocket and emptied out a trickle of coppers.

"Aye, Sam, *I'm* one of the villains you heard me speaking of, and all I do is sing out the word 'thief' and every one of 'em points me straight to his money, sure as a compass points north." She laughed again and flung the emptied purses into the fire.

"Aye, and it's only *after* they've reached for 'em that I finger their pouches. Let 'em discover it when they stop for a meal, and blame the man next to 'em. Or when they pull in somewhere else for the night. But they'll remember it clear that they checked their purses before leaving the Half-a-Moon Inn, and still had 'em with 'em."

She counted the money in her hand once again, and stood warming herself by the fire.

"Oh, me hands move fast, lad, quick as swifts and swallows. But they're dishonest hands, you understand, and me great-great-grandfather who built this house was a worthy judge and an *honest* man—may his soul rot in heaven! Oh, he laid up these chimneys with his own honest hands—and built a curse into 'em as well, lest any of his thieving brothers should snatch the house for himself when he died. Aye, for it's only *honest* hands that can get the wood to catch in the grates. *Your* hands, lad!"

Miss Grackle cackled like a hen. "The last of me boys ran off quick as a ghost at sunrise, he did—and froze to death in the bargain. So ever since the air's turned cold I've been having to rely on the guests to build fires. But here you blow in with the first of the snow—aye, you turn up handy as a thimble, boy. Now, pitch another load of logs on the grate and then back to sleep with you. You'll need it for tonight, lad, believe me."

Aaron built up the blaze and climbed upstairs, his feet still stinging and sore. He searched for his boots without success, sat by the window and stared outside. It was snowing again.

How had he gotten himself into such a fix? Could his mother truly have abandoned him, as Miss Grackle had suggested? Or was she waiting for him at home right now, wondering what in the world had become of him? He'd been so certain he'd find her that he hadn't thought to leave a note in the house. Yet surely she'd be out hunting for him at this very moment. But was she searching the wrong road, or combing the wrong town?

Anxiously Aaron peered out at the road, following it with his eyes until it vanished among the trees. Somehow he had to get free of Miss Grackle—and suddenly he spotted her, walking out toward a little shed set apart from the house. Aaron saw she was carrying the empty woodbox, to refill it no doubt— and knew that he hadn't a moment to spare.

He ripped the covers off his bed, and wrapped each of his feet in a blanket. If only he could get away from the inn, he could climb up a tree out of the snow, and wait for a traveler to come down the road. Quick as he could, Aaron scurried down the stairs, poked his head out from the stairway and saw that the coast was clear. With his heart beating furiously, he dashed to the door, threw it open—and stood face to face with Miss Grackle.

"Well now—what have we here!" She hoisted him

up by the shirt collar, walked inside with him and slammed the door shut.

"Still got a mind to run off, have you, me ungrateful scamp?" She dropped him down on the floor and picked up her switch off the mantel. "Aye, I knew what you'd be up to, me minnow. All me boys try it—once."

She pinned him to the floor, unwrapped the blankets and brought the willow down on his feet with all her might. Aaron jerked with the pain, desperately trying to get free.

"Aye, Sam, I'll whip some manners into you yet. Believe me I will." Time after time the switch hummed through the air and stung at his feet. Aaron squirmed like a fish and soon grew too exhausted to struggle against her. At last she was satisfied.

"Now up on your feet, boy, and hop to your room! Quick now!"

Aaron picked himself up onto his knees, and painfully rose to his feet. They had already begun to swell, and they felt as tender as ripe tomatoes. Slowly, laboriously, he made his way toward the stairs, wincing with every step.

"And if you've still got a mind to run off down the road, I'll whip you again till it'll be all you can do to crawl like a baby. Now begone with you!"

It seemed like ages to Aaron before he finished

climbing the stairs. At last he entered his room, Miss Grackle charging upstairs behind him, slamming the door shut and turning a key in the lock. His feet throbbing, Aaron shuffled weakly across the floor, collapsed on his bed and fell thankfully to sleep.

6

It was late afternoon when Aaron awoke. Hooves clattered outside, and he pricked up his ears at the sound of voices below. The guests had begun to arrive.

Immediately, he thought of dashing outside and taking off on a horse—and then he remembered his feet. They were puffy and red and striped from the lashing, and they felt swollen to twice their size. Gently, he placed them on the floor, gradually shifted his weight onto them and slowly hobbled toward the window. All of a sudden there came a booming up the stairs and Miss Grackle burst in through the door.

"Back to your chores now—quick, boy!" She grabbed hold of his wrist and yanked him down the long flight of stairs, Aaron howling inside with pain.

"To the fire with you, boy, and put some more blood in its veins! Let me hear it spit like a cat and curse like a drunkard—and be brisk about it!"

She hauled him, stumbling behind her, across the room, threw him down before the hearth and stirred the pot of soup hanging over the grate. "And if you still be having trouble remembering your manners, why I'll be happy to remind 'em to you," she said with a smile, and picked up the willow switch off the mantel and put it down once again.

Slowly, Aaron built up the fire. He listened for the sound of horses and watched the callers stride in through the door and stamp the snow off their feet.

"Welcome, me fine gentlemen," Miss Grackle called out. "Inside with you, me worthies, and thaw out your bones—and there's hot soup and dumplings waiting for you as well." She brought out six loaves of bread she'd baked while Aaron was asleep, distributed them around the tables and continued bustling about, collecting her fees, bringing out the dishes, stirring the soup.

"Up now, boy," she hissed into Aaron's ear, "and serve the gentlemen their soup."

Aaron rose slowly to his feet, ladled out the soup

47

and painfully made his way about the room, setting the bowls in front of the guests. He looked into their faces but recognized no one, and when all the callers had received their soup, Miss Grackle sat him down beside her, apart from the others.

"Just look at 'em," she muttered, indicating the guests. "A pack of beggars and rascals, wouldn't you say, Sam?"

Aaron nodded his head.

"Aye, lad, that's the most of 'em for certain, and too poor to be worth the bother of plucking their purses. But that ain't the *whole* of 'em, lad. Nay, boy, there's more to 'em than that. And I'll take you into me confidence, I will, and tell you a secret."

Her eyes grew wide and excited, her voice dropped down to a whisper. "There's men of wealth sitting before us, Sam, men that live in great manors with more rooms than you could count, with flocks of servants scurrying about 'em like mice. Aye, lad, could be there's noble blood among 'em tonight, lords and earls, and dukes as well!"

Aaron peered at the guests in amazement. They dribbled soup down their chins and onto their chests, each man guarding his bowl like a dog with a bone. Could these be the manners of dukes and earls?

"Naturally, they're dressed up like kings when

they're home in their castles. But when they have to go traveling from one place to another, why they get up in rags like these ones here, lest the thieves and scoundrels cluster about 'em like flies. Me own sharp-witted mother reasoned it out herself, and spent the whole of her life just waiting to snare such a one. Oh, they're a crafty lot, they are, but I've got me a trick for sniffing 'em out, and you can help me with it, too, me little nuthatch. Now get some food into you, boy—and mind you stay clear of the dumplings."

Aaron moved his feet slowly across the room to the fireplace, ladled out a bowlful of soup and sat down by himself near the fire. He wondered why she'd ordered him to keep away from the dumplings, but before he could begin eating, one of the guests called out for more, and Miss Grackle commanded him to fill the man's bowl.

"Me compliments on the soup," the man said to Miss Grackle. "Sturdiest soup I ever come across."

Miss Grackle put a dainty smile on her face. "Too kind, sir, too kind. And to give you the truth of the matter, any praise for the food belongs to the boy there."

Aaron turned and looked at her in surprise. What had he done besides peel the potatoes? He brought the man his steaming bowl and sat himself down to his own, stirring it slowly to let it cool, puzzling over Miss Grackle's remark.

"Me compliments to the both of ye, then," the man continued. "But have you heard the news of Lord Tom, good madam?"

Instantly, Aaron's ears pricked up.

"Escaped out of prison he did, so they say. Burst the chains round his arms as though they were thread, and gnawed through the chains on his feet with his teeth. Run off back to the woods, they say, and a tidy reward waiting for any that knows where he is."

Aaron's eyes bulged with terror, but Miss Grackle looked perfectly calm.

"And who," she asked, "is Lord Tom?"

Aaron gaped in amazement. Surely Miss Grackle of all people would have heard of him—and suddenly he began trembling inside at the thought that he'd strayed so far from home as to find himself in a land where Lord Tom's terrible deeds were unknown.

"The fellow's a highwayman, madam," the caller replied. "Hunts his prey down in Bingham Woods, with a long-barreled pistol and a temper as short as your little finger."

Miss Grackle remained unimpressed. "The woods are plenty full of brigands as it is," she declared. "Can't see that one more's worth troubling about."

She walked to the hearth, and ladled herself out a bowlful of soup. "Aye, he'll have plenty of company among the trees, I warrant, and ought to feel himself right at home." She gave the soup a stir, picked up her bowl and carried it over to the far end of the room.

Aaron looked at her in wonderment, pondering her ignorance of Lord Tom. At last his soup had cooled and Aaron sampled a mouthful—and spit it back out as quick as he could. Scraps of cowhide floated about in it! The broth tasted of leather, and he found a tack among the vegetables—Miss Grackle must have sliced up his boots and thrown them in the soup!

He reached for a loaf of bread, broke off a piece— and found that it tasted of wool. His stockings!

Now he knew perfectly well what she'd meant when she'd given him credit for the meal. He shot her a furious glance and caught her dabbing her lips with his very own handkerchief, the one his mother herself had embroidered for him. The light-fingered scoundrel had snatched that from him as well, and had decided to keep it for herself! She returned Aaron's stare with a knowing smile, and he angrily dumped his soup back in the pot and remained by the fire, jabbing at the logs with the poker.

One by one the callers finished their dinners, and

Miss Grackle set Aaron to clearing the tables and washing the dishes. He kept his ears cocked to their conversation, straining for any information he might pick up. At last they began to grow sleepy and yawn, and gradually they trooped up to bed.

"Now we wait a bit," said Miss Grackle when the last one had gone, and she sat him down next to her, listening to every sound from above. When the ceiling had long since ceased to creak from the guests' footsteps, and long after Miss Grackle poked her head out the door and saw that the third-story window was dark, she cautiously led Aaron up the stairs and into the callers' room.

She stood in the doorway awhile, making sure all were asleep. Then she stepped inside, pulling Aaron behind her, and drew a chair up to one of the beds. He watched in amazement as she bent over the face of the man who'd so enjoyed the soup, carefully took hold of his eyelid, slowly peeled it back—and there, lit up in the darkness, was the man's dream!

"Aye, Sam, it's the dumplings that put the light in their visions and keep 'em sleeping deep as dead men as well. Me own special recipe, it is, and a handy one at that. Oh, for they may look like beggars when they walk through the door, but when a duke dreams of home, lad, he'll be wearing silken robes and rubies on his fingers, and eating roast goose and not gruel."

Aaron peered in astonishment at the dream dancing across the man's eye—and realized Miss Grackle had looked into his own the same way.

"And if you find us any royalty," Miss Grackle continued, "we won't even bother with lifting his purse, but take him prisoner instead, and ransom him back for a wagonload of gold. Aye, and move into a manor ourselves. Now pull up a chair to that one yonder—and keep your eyeballs sharp for silks and jewels!"

Aaron did as she said, pulled back the man's lid and watched the fantasies float across his eye like clouds through the sky. Perhaps one of the guests had seen his mother in Craftsbury, or passed her somewhere along the road—perhaps she'd turn up in the background of a dream.

For hours Aaron combed through the callers' visions, carefully searching for just a glimpse of his mother, or their horse, or merely the sea. He saw pigs with wings and wagons that sped along without horses, but nothing of what he was looking for, and no sign of lords or ladies.

Far into the night they looked into dreams, Aaron's stomach rumbling with hunger and his eyes growing heavy as gold doubloons. When Miss Grackle herself began to yawn, she led him to her bedroom and had him build her a fire. Then she marched him down the hall to his own room, where he dropped straight into sleep before she could turn the key in the lock.

7

Day after day Aaron tended the fires at the Half-a-Moon Inn, penned up inside for the lack of his boots, longing to be home. He'd searched the house from top to bottom, but there wasn't a spare pair of shoes to be found. And even if there were, Miss Grackle rarely let him out of her sight, except when she locked him in his room to nap in the afternoon and when she slept a few hours before dawn. And if he did spot a chance to make his escape, how could he be sure she wasn't waiting just out the door, with her willow switch raised at hand?

Sometimes, when he was sent up to sleep in the afternoons, Aaron would sit by the window, gazing out at the snow lying thick on the ground, waiting for his mother to come into view. Would she never come looking for him? Had she given up searching the woods for a sign of him? Was she combing the coastline instead? Or had she never made her way home?

He kept his ears cocked to every word spoken by the guests, always listening for the sound of her name. At night he picked through their dreams with care, studying every figure in every crowd, searching not for men of noble blood, but only for a glimpse of her face.

He looked longingly into the eyes of the guests when he served them, but none of them paid him any mind. He wanted to jump up and down and wave his arms about madly, but Miss Grackle would no doubt explain it as a case of brain fever, lock him in his room—and whip him for it later. His pen and ink had been in the sack that had disappeared, so there was no way of writing—until he realized one morning how his hands got so black while building the fires. From the charcoal, of course!

Quickly, he stuck a piece in his pocket while Miss Grackle's head was turned. And when she went to the shed to bring in more wood, he feverishly tore off a piece of wallpaper from behind a bureau, wrote out a plea for help and hid it in his shirt. When Miss

Grackle returned and the callers came down, Aaron deftly stuck the note into one of their coat pockets and hoped for the best. But before the man managed to slip out the door, Miss Grackle had snatched up his coin purse—and Aaron's note along with it.

"Oh, but you'll have to be quicker than that," she snarled, when the last of the guests had left. She waved the note tauntingly in his face and threw it in the fire.

"Me ignorant eyes may not be able to read, but they seen what you were about, me sparrow. Putting things *into* their pockets rather than taking 'em out."

She took up her switch, yanked him over to a table and brought it humming down through the air and across his fingers.

"Taken a fancy to scribbling, have you? Well then, put your talents to good use, boy, and give the sign a new coat of paint, lest any royalty mistake us for no more than a house—and be quick with it!"

She smacked his hands with the switch once again and set him free. "And if there be so much as a line that's not straight or a brush hair out of place, why I'll whip your fingers again till they do the job right."

She stormed out the door, took the sign off its hooks, and brought him paint and a brush. Aaron's fingers throbbed and stung as he scraped off the old paint and laboriously began painting the sign anew. He could barely manage to hold the brush, much less guide it precisely, and it seemed like hours before the sign was completed.

"That'll do," snapped Miss Grackle, running her eyes over it quickly. "Now hop to the potatoes, boy, quick now. And feed the blaze there some wood, before I serve you up to it for lunch meself."

"The fool!" Aaron thought to himself, and secretly smiled through the rest of his chores. He could barely keep himself from bursting out laughing when Miss Grackle found the sign to be dry and hung it back up on its hooks. The moon in the corner was there as before, but the words now read: HELP! AARON PATRICK HERE! MISS GRACKLE A PICKPOCKET!

Oh, but he'd be rid of her soon enough now. This very evening, if not before!

Aaron was too restless to sleep when he climbed upstairs for his nap, and he trembled with excitement when Miss Grackle brought him down once again and set him to warming the house for the arrival of the guests. All afternoon he'd listened for horses, and when the callers finally began to arrive, Aaron ran to the window and watched them approach.

One after another, they tied up their horses,

walked up the steps—and strode past the sign as though it didn't exist. Aaron searched their faces in desperation when they came through the door, but the travelers ignored him as usual. He looked into their eyes when he served them their soup and watched in amazement as they devoured their dinners, gathered by the fire and trooped up to bed just as always—and realized it at last. They identified the inn by the moon on the sign. None of the guests could read.

That night a furious snowstorm blew out of the sky. The wind whipped madly about the house, pouncing on the roof and flinging snow against the shutters. At dawn Aaron awoke and looked out his window—and there, riding on horseback, a caped figure with long brown hair approached.

Aaron's eyes froze wide open, gaping in disbelief. It was his mother.

At last, she'd come to fetch him home again! He jumped to his feet and scrambled into his clothes. His door had already been unlocked and Aaron dashed across the room, flew down the stairs—and was snatched up at the door by Miss Grackle herself.

"Company's coming, me little titmouse, and a familiar face at that, though we ain't never been properly introduced." She grabbed hold of Aaron and hauled him back upstairs, kicking and squirming. "And there's nothing company hates worse than a pesky boy hanging about."

She threw him in a closet, locked the door and bustled back downstairs.

Aaron crouched down on his knees and put his ear to the floor. He could make out the sound of approaching hooves, then steps on the porch, then a knock at the door. Miss Grackle's steps boomed across the floor, the door creaked open and slammed shut with a bang.

"Pardon me, madam, but could it be you've caught sight of a boy in a plaid wool coat a-wandering out this way? A mute boy he is, that and my own dear son."

It was his mother's voice for certain—Aaron knew it at once. But why had she bothered to ask? She could read the sign out front, she *knew* he was here!

"A mute boy, you say?" Miss Grackle replied, musing. "Well now, let me consider the matter a moment."

There was a pause.

"A plaid coat, you say?"

"Yes, that's right," said his mother.

"Well now. Then it's a mute boy with a plaid coat we be looking for, isn't it now?"

"Exactly."

There was another pause.

"Well now, come to think of it, I don't believe I've come across any such article. I do have a boy here that helps with the chores, but he just jabbers away all the day long like a finch. Couldn't say he's mute, in the proper sense of the word."

"I see," said his mother. What was she waiting for? Wasn't she going to *demand* that Miss Grackle hand him over at once? Aaron jumped up and down on the floor as hard as he could and Miss Grackle began sneezing—he must have shaken the dust loose from the ceiling.

"Aye, he's upstairs right now, tacking down a new carpet for me. Handy with the tools, he is."

"I see," said his mother.

"But I'll keep me eyes sharp for him, madam. Scamper off from home, did he now? Oh, but just let him get a taste of the cold and he'll be back soon enough, believe me he will."

There was a pause.

"Well now," said his mother, "I suppose it isn't likely I'd turn him up out in this direction anyway. But if you should come by him, I'd be greatly obliged if you'd send him toward Hifton Head with one of your travelers. Most humbly obliged indeed."

Was she actually going to leave, then? Aaron jumped on the floor with all his might and pounded on the walls with his fists.

"Without a moment's delay," Miss Grackle replied. "You can depend on it."

He could hear steps moving across the floor, felt the front door close and heard the neigh of a horse. Hadn't she heard him? Why was she leaving him? He pounded against the door until he was exhausted. What was the matter with her?

He stopped to listen, and caught the sound of hooves fading away. He pounded at the door one last time and crumpled down on the floor, tears silently moving down his cheeks. A half hour later Miss Grackle unlocked the door and fetched him downstairs.

"Strike flint, boy, and hoist the flames up high!" She flung a shawl over her shoulders and clutched it tight. "Take the ice out of this chillful air, Sam, and then hop to the potatoes."

Miss Grackle bustled about the room, stepped out onto the porch for a minute and returned with a shiver.

"Curse the wind!" she hissed. "Could have just cost us some royal company."

Aaron looked up at her quizzically.

"Hurry up with the blaze, boy—it's nothing. Just the sign out front. Wind blew it down during the night."

Aaron stopped what he was doing, and suddenly knew what had happened. The sign must have fallen facedown on the ground—his mother had never seen it.

8

All day long Aaron wandered sullenly about the house like a homeless spirit. He looked out the window while he tended to his chores, watching the wind drive the clouds across the sky.

Would his mother ever bother to search this road again? Was that the last look he'd ever get of her, the last time he'd ever hear the sound of her voice? Somehow he had to slip out of Miss Grackle's grasp, or she'd have him striking flint to her fires for the rest of his days.

That evening, while Aaron was serving the guests, wagon wheels creaked to a halt outside, footsteps thumped heavily up onto the porch, Aaron turned to look as the door swung open—and there stood the ragman.

"Bless me bats!" he burst out. "It's me quiet little friend."

Aaron's eyes lit up and suddenly he felt weightless with joy and relief. At last he'd been rescued! Why, he'd be home straightaway—in a few days at the most!

He trembled with excitement, and in his haste to run to the ragman he spilled a bowl of hot soup and dumplings down the front of a guest, a huge man who promptly let out a cry.

"*Curse* you, you clumsy scamp!" he shouted. He wore a leather eye patch and focused all his anger into a fearsome one-eyed glare.

"On purpose, was it?" he snarled, staring straight at Aaron. "I ought to have your *head* for it, boy—and maybe I will!"

"Quick, boy!" barked Miss Grackle. "Fetch a rag and clean the worthy gentleman's clothes." He did as she said while the man muttered ominously to himself. Then Aaron brought him another bowl of soup and fled to the ragman.

"Well met, me lad," said the ragman with a smile. "Well met indeed." He sat himself down at a table and Aaron served him his dinner.

"Decided to stay on as an errand boy, have you?

Fine choice, me lad. Excellent choice." Aaron strenuously shook his head no, but the ragman seemed not to notice.

"Fine training, it is. Good experience for a boy—aye, and I'm sure your mistress is grateful indeed to have a polite and well-mannered lad such as yourself. One that knows how to hold his tongue before his elders."

Hold his tongue? Would the man never understand that Aaron was mute, and that he was trying to escape from the inn? Aaron tugged on the ragman's sleeve, desperate to get the truth into his head before Miss Grackle should intervene, but the man's mind was as impenetrable as stone.

"Aye, I worked at an inn once meself, as a boy. That I did, with the travelers always coming and going, and the stories of all the places they've seen. No better place for a boy to learn about life."

Aaron struggled to make himself understood by the ragman, shaking his head back and forth, making faces of pain, pointing fearfully toward Miss Grackle. But before he could get his point across, Miss Grackle called him away and set him to clearing the tables. Somehow he had to get back to the ragman, but the moment Aaron finished one chore Miss Grackle gave him another, and he watched in dismay as the first of the guests began tramping upstairs—the ragman among them.

Aaron worked his mind feverishly, determined not to let the chance slip through his fingers. Yet Miss Grackle seemed suspicious, never letting him out of her sight, and when they entered the guests' room to sift through their dreams, it was Miss Grackle who pulled up next to the ragman, sitting Aaron down by the man who'd cursed him earlier.

He felt restless and jumpy, with no patience for searching for silks and jewels, but he tried to pretend that nothing was out of the ordinary. He pulled the lid back from the man's uncovered eye—and instantly a chill shot up his spine like lightning. The man was dreaming of creeping slowly down a hall, entering a room where a boy slept in a bed, and with a vengeful smile, driving a knife into his back. And the boy was none other than Aaron himself!

Aaron looked closer, trembling with fear, and saw that the man had no patch over his eye in the dream, and sported a wild red beard, just like Lord Tom's. Aaron looked again, and gaped in horror. It *was* Lord Tom he was dreaming of—and suddenly Aaron began to shake. The eye he was looking at was brown. Carefully he lifted up the patch over the other eye, and let it down again in a hurry. The eye behind it was perfectly normal—and as blue as the sea. Lord Tom himself was lying before him!

Aaron's heart began racing like a runaway horse.

Of all the people to spill a bowl of soup onto, why had he picked Lord Tom? He must have shaved off his beard and strapped on an eye patch so as not to be spotted, and left Bingham Woods for lands where he wasn't yet known. Aaron stared at his face, imagining it with a beard, and recognized it as the face that had haunted him so.

Was he planning to put an end to Aaron for his clumsiness this very night? He'd killed men for less, Aaron was certain of that. Or since he'd know just where to find him, would he save Aaron for the future, and murder him at his leisure? Somehow he had to see that the man was locked up, and in a desperate hurry.

There was no hope of getting the guests to understand. And Miss Grackle herself had never heard of the man. Suddenly an idea burst into his head.

He shot up from his chair, ran to Miss Grackle and tugged on her arm, pointing excitedly toward Lord Tom.

"What is it, me little bedbug? Did you see something, Sam?"

Aaron nodded his head wildly, and pantomimed a man admiring rings on his fingers.

"Well, what is it then, lad—have you struck noble blood?"

Aaron nodded his head, and Miss Grackle jumped to her feet in a flash.

"Quick, Sam, what manner of man have you found us? A duke, is it, boy?"

Aaron shook his head no, and quickly imitated a man walking with a great full-length robe trailing behind him.

"By the gods!" Miss Grackle exclaimed, her eyes bulging with greedy excitement. "Can it be you've uncovered a prince?"

Aaron shook his head again, and pretended to place a glittering crown on his head.

"Great heavens, boy—is it a king, then?"

Frantically Aaron nodded his head yes.

"A king under me own roof?" Miss Grackle burst out. "Impossible!" She scrambled madly across the room, bent over Lord Tom a moment and straightened up again.

"It's gone, boy—the dream's changed." She grabbed Aaron by the shoulders and scrutinized his face.

"But you say you saw it for yourself?" she asked, her eyes wide and alert.

Aaron nodded wildly, straining to look as excited as he could.

"And you're certain he had a crown, are you, Sam?"

He nodded again.

"Well now, maybe you've struck something after all, boy." Her eyes sparkled hungrily, and a calculating smile spread over her face. "What did I tell you, lad, but there's all manner of royalty just waiting to be found. And a king at that!"

She hovered over the man like a hawk, trembling with visions of wagons full of gold. "Oh, you've done well, you have, and I'm right proud of you, Sam. And I'll see to it that you get a wing all to yourself when we get us a castle. You can depend on it, lad."

Aaron tried to look as greedy and pleased as she, and watched as she pawed through the man's possessions, picked out his pistol and stuck it in her apron pocket.

"We'll lead him down in the cellar tomorrow morning, give him a shove and lock the door behind him. And you, Sam, can write out some proper ransom notes. Then it's just a matter of passing the time till the gold arrives and His Majesty goes free—and we begin living like kings ourselves!"

Aaron sighed with relief inside at the thought of Lord Tom locked safely away in the cellar, and hoped for once that her scheme went as planned. Now all he need do was to figure a way to escape before Miss Grackle discovered that it was a rogue she was boarding, rather than royalty. He worked his mind desperately while he was led to his room, and lay awake through the night, too restless to sleep.

Slowly the sky began to lighten in the east, and soon Miss Grackle marched down the hallway, unlocked his door and stuck her head inside.

"Into your clothes, and to the grates with you, Sam!" Aaron dressed in a hurry, hopping from one bare foot to the other on the icy floor. Suddenly he began to question his plan, wondering how long Lord Tom would stay cooped up in the cellar. There'd be no queens or princes to bail *him* out! Why, he'd be mad as fifty hornets and likely burst down the door himself—and leave knives in *both* their backs as payment for his keep.

Quickly Aaron scurried downstairs and set about kindling a fire, knowing he had to get free of the inn without a moment to spare.

"Give us a blaze now, Sam, and one fit for a king!" Miss Grackle whispered hoarsely. "Our guest of honor isn't used to waking up to a chill in the air—so raise up the flames and make him feel right at home."

Aaron finished arranging the logs on the grate, struck a spark from the flint—but couldn't get the wood shavings to catch.

"Quick, Sam, a fire—I can already hear feet stirring above."

Aaron struck at the flint time and again, but the tinder refused to burn.

"What is it now, me little termite?" Miss Grackle hissed with impatience. She stood over him clutching a shawl around her shoulders, her teeth chattering furiously. "The flames *always* come when you call 'em. Now bring 'em up, boy!"

Nervously, Aaron arranged the tinder anew, shifted the wood about and struck the flint again. The spark jumped forward into the wood shavings—and immediately died out.

"How can it be?" asked Miss Grackle in puzzlement. Then all of a sudden she swooped down upon him and yanked him up by the wrist.

"Unless it be the case that you've done something *dishonest!*"

She shook him by the arm and peered into his face. "Quick now, boy—explain yourself!"

Aaron squirmed in her grasp like a snake, his mind whirling in confusion—and then he remembered. The lie that he'd told her about Lord Tom's dream—*that's* why the wood wouldn't catch! There was no turning back now—he had to escape!

"Out with it, boy—before I squeeze it out of you meself!" She tightened her grip on his wrist till the bones were ready to snap.

"Stolen something, is it? Put poison in me food? Is it lies ye be telling, me ungrateful scamp?"

Aaron writhed in desperation, feverishly working his brain for an excuse—when the sound of footsteps on stairs echoed down from above.

"Enough—" whispered Miss Grackle, and she threw him down on the floor. "Quick now, to the potatoes with you, and keep still and out of the way. I'll finish with you in a moment!"

One by one the callers came clumping downstairs. Miss Grackle took up her post by the door, explained that the chimney flue wasn't working, lectured them on thieves as usual and bid them farewell.

"Well met, me lad," called the ragman as he headed toward the door. "Aye, I can see you're working hard, and making your mistress right proud of you too. Just as quiet and polite a lad as they come, and never so much as a peep out of you. For me, it's homeward to Williford. Farewell now, me lad!"

Aaron waved good-bye, longing to dash out the door with him—but Miss Grackle flashed him a look that kept him bolted to his seat. But no sooner had the ragman stepped out the door than there was a commotion above, feet came crashing downstairs, and Lord Tom appeared in full fury.

"Where's me pistol, now!" he shouted in a rage. "Hand it over—brisk now!"

There were no other travelers left inside, and Miss Grackle looked at the man in surprise and stepped forward from the door.

"Your firearm, is it, me worthy gentleman? Missing? Most lamentable—and just as I was discussing the subject of theft."

Lord Tom paid her no mind, rummaging about the room for his gun and cursing under his breath.

"No doubt one of the other guests has already sped off down the road with it. A shame, sir, and an excellent pistol I'm sure it was. But as it happens I've a fine pair of dueling irons handed down from me grandfather. And as I've no use for 'em meself, and to make up for your loss, I should like you to take 'em. I insist on it, sir."

Lord Tom stopped his searching. "Well now, and where might *they* be?" he snarled.

"Why, just down the stairs here—let me show you." Miss Grackle led him to a door at the far end of the room, took a key from her pocket and turned it in the latch. She swung the door open and motioned for him to precede her.

"A fine pair of pistols, I promise you, sir. Just sitting in the cellar collecting dust," she said, her voice fading as she stepped down the stairs right behind him.

"Now!" Aaron thought—and he dashed across the room and out the door. He saw that the ragman hadn't yet left, skipped through the snow to his wagon and scrambled into the back. Only the presence of a king could have taken Miss Grackle's eyes off him, and a moment later he heard the door swing open.

"Sam! Step forward! Before I lose my patience!"

Aaron buried himself out of sight under the rags, and realized that the ragman had been inspecting his horse and hadn't noticed him climb into the back. Again and again Miss Grackle shouted for him. Aaron froze in place beneath the rags, cursing the ragman for taking so long, when all of a sudden the whip snapped, the wagon jerked—and he was off!

9

Down the road they went, while Miss Grackle shrieked for Aaron from the doorway. Oh, she could spit tacks and split her lungs yelling—but she wouldn't fetch him this time!

Her voice faded in the distance as the ragman drove on, unaware of whom he had with him. Snow began falling and Aaron wrapped his feet in rags, burrowed in deeper out of the cold and decided to wait till he was well away from the Half-a-Moon Inn before coming out of hiding.

All morning long he rode in the wagon, as snug as a chipmunk. Sometime after noon the wagon came to a halt, and Aaron heard the ragman climb down.

He listened for a while, then cautiously poked his head out of the rags and saw that they'd stopped at an inn in a town he'd never seen, and realized that the ragman must have gone in for a meal.

Aaron rose out of the pile of rags, climbed down from the wagon and headed toward the door, when it swung open and the ragman charged out in a fearsome rage. When he saw Aaron before him he stopped in his tracks, then sprang forward like a cat and grabbed him roughly by the arms.

"Bless me bats! First me money disappears, then *you* turn up. Stowed away in me wagon, have ye? And picked me pocket as well?" He gave Aaron a mighty shake.

"Where's me silver, boy—quick now, before I break you up into kindling!"

Aaron squirmed in his grasp, frightened and confused—and then realized that Miss Grackle must have lifted the man's purse before he'd managed to slip out the door.

"The thieves and cutthroats are thick as flies—and I should have known you for one the moment I set eyes on you."

Aaron couldn't believe that the ragman had changed so toward him, and then remembered how suspiciously he'd acted the first time they'd met.

"Got it hid then, have you?" the ragman shouted.

He searched Aaron's clothes, scowled and shook him angrily again. "Or is it tucked away in the back now, me suckling pickpocket?"

He climbed into the wagon and rooted among the rags for it. "Oh, but I learned me lesson with you, me little scamp. And if you're looking for mercy on account of your age, *I'll* show you mercy, boy—with the edge of me knife. Now where's me money!"

Suddenly Aaron spotted a stick on the ground, picked it up and drew a likeness of Miss Grackle in the snow, clutching a coin purse in her hand. The ragman's eyebrows jerked up when he saw it.

"What's your meaning, lad—that *she's* the one that's plucked it?"

Aaron nodded desperately.

"Will you wager your heartbeat on it, boy?"

He nodded again.

"Why, the thieving fingersmith. That's all the money I own! Oh, but I'll shake the larceny out of her good and proper. Quick boy, into the wagon with you!"

Aaron scrambled aboard, and trembled to see the ragman heading back toward the Half-a-Moon Inn. He'd rather have shaken hands with the devil himself than set eyes on Miss Grackle again, and he cursed himself sharply for not thinking of that sooner.

81

Onward they drove, with the wind and snow whipping down from the sky. Soon they were plodding along at a porcupine's pace, struggling merely to keep a hold on the road. They lowered their heads to the freezing wind, while the snow swirled through the air and clawed at their faces. Finally the road grew too difficult to travel, and they sought shelter at the first house they came to.

For three days and nights the blizzard raged. The wind howled like a pack of wild dogs, the snow streamed down without end. The temperature plunged, colder than Aaron had ever felt in his life, and the snow put a stop to all travel on the roads.

Finally the weather cleared, the snow began to melt and Aaron was distressed to see the ragman ready to press on. Aaron tried his best to skip free of the man, but the ragman still had his suspicions of Aaron and kept watch over the boy like a jailer.

The snow was deep when they finally headed toward the inn, and though the distance was short, it was evening before they arrived. All the windows were dark, and the house looked deserted. A single horse stood out front in the blackness.

"You'd best not have been juggling the truth about me purse," the ragman bellowed, "or I'll reach down your throat and pull your heart up like a carrot."

Aaron had to be dragged out of the wagon by the arm, struggling not to be returned to Miss Grackle. The two of them crept through the front door, stepped inside and stood perfectly still in the darkness. The air was like ice. Footsteps creaked on the floor above them. The ragman listened for a moment, pulled a candle from his pocket and lit it—and there was Miss Grackle, and Lord Tom right beside her, sitting before the hearth, frozen solid as stone!

"Bless me bats!" gasped the ragman. A mountain of logs lay on the grate, but the wood had not burned. She must have been stranded alone when the storm closed the roads—and frozen for the lack of a fire! She'd even brought Lord Tom out of the cellar to try and raise the flames—and found out how honest a man *he* was!

Aaron stared at her in wonder, reached inside her huge apron pocket and with a sigh of relief pulled out the ragman's purse. With no flames in the fireplace she'd had no chance to burn it.

"There now, that's what we be looking for. Thank you, boy." Aaron was in no mood to linger and pressed the ragman to leave. But just as they turned to go, footsteps descended the staircase, a figure approached, the ragman held out his candle—and there stood Aaron's mother.

"Aaron, my lad!" He stared at her in disbelief as she swept across the room toward him, wrapped him inside her cape and hugged him close.

"Oh, but I knew I'd find you here somewhere, my dove." Aaron's eyes glittered with joy while his mind spun in bafflement, unable to understand how she could be here.

"This icy one here told me so herself," she said, indicating Miss Grackle. "When I showed up a-looking for you, and she commenced a-wheezing into *this*." She dipped into Miss Grackle's pocket and plucked out Aaron's handkerchief. But of course—when he'd jumped up and down in the closet and loosened the dust, she must have clapped it to her nose when she was sneezing!

"Half a glimpse was all that I got of it, and never even took it for my own needlework. But when I got home and went through your clothes and found one of your handkerchiefs missing—why the sight of it flashed in my eyes like lightning. Oh, I knew then for certain that she knew more than she was telling, and quick as I could I came to pay her another visit. And see what I found!"

She hugged Aaron again, and glanced down at the rags on his feet.

"But where are your boots, my dove? Ah, but they were cramping your toes as it was."

She disappeared out the door, and returned with a

pair of new-made, knee-length boots, shiny black and smelling of leather.

"These are what kept me in Craftsbury so long—'twas deep in the night before Mr. Cheedle, the cobbler, put the last tack in 'em. And then the snow came down, and the wagon got stuck—oh, I don't blame you for leaving. Come looking for me, did you?"

Aaron nodded his head.

"Well, you did the right thing, lad. I could have used your help, and as it was I had to keep myself warm in the wool that I'd bought and live on the food that I was carrying home. But enough of that now—and happy birthday to you, boy!"

She handed him the boots, and Aaron's eyes lit up.

"Your birthday, is it?" the ragman asked.

Aaron nodded his head and unwrapped the rags from his feet, while the ragman walked out to his wagon and brought back a pair of wool stockings that were practically new.

"Can't have you going about barefoot in your boots, can we?" the ragman asked with a smile.

"Certainly not," said his mother. "Try 'em on, then, lad."

Aaron slipped into the socks, pulled on the boots and stamped his feet into them. He stretched his toes and strode across the room. They felt grand.

"Yes, indeed," said his mother, "they're more appropriate to a boy who'll be taking the wagon into Craftsbury by himself soon enough."

Aaron's ears pricked up and he smiled excitedly at the thought.

"But now tell me, my dove—what became of my coat?"

Aaron thought for a moment, then reached into Miss Grackle's apron pocket and pulled out her key ring. He took the candle from the ragman, led the way up to her bedroom and unlocked her closet door, to find his mother's coat as well as his own, and his burlap sack with the rest of his belongings.

"Took your boots and stockings away in the cold of the winter, and your wool coat as well?" Aaron's mother asked. "Why, the woman deserved to freeze, I warrant. But who's that beside her?"

Aaron took his pen and ink from his sack and wrote out "Lord Tom" on a piece of paper.

"By the heavens, lad—can it be?"

Aaron nodded his head, led them downstairs and removed the patch from his eye.

"It's true!" gasped his mother. "Why, they've been combing Bingham Woods for the man and trembling in their beds, and here you've got him sitting by the hearth, frozen stiff as a log. You'll be famous, my dove—and with a reward just a-waiting for you!"

Aaron glowed with his good fortune and proudly led the three of them out of the inn.

"Aye, madam, I'd be proud to have me such a son meself," said the ragman. "Just as quiet and polite and well brung up as they come."

He climbed up on his wagon and bid them farewell. "Homeward to Williford," he called out into the night, and he snapped his whip and was off down the road.

Slowly, Aaron and his mother walked over to their horse. He strapped down his sack, and his mother stuck her foot in the stirrup and hoisted herself up.

"You take the reins," she said, holding them out to Aaron.

He smiled, climbed up in front of her and looked about. The woods were knee-deep in snow, the night air was still. He listened to a bird chirping in the distance. Then he flicked the reins, leaning back against his mother, and headed the horse for home.

Turn the page to read
an excerpt from the sequel:

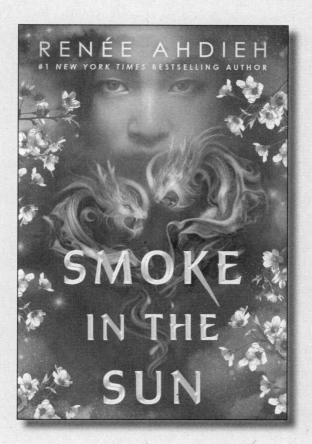

ᴛall and ᴘroud and ʜapless

This was a scene from a story she'd heard before.

A young woman in her rightful place, ensconced at the Golden Castle. Betrothed to the son of the emperor's favorite consort. Bestowing honor to the Hattori name.

The scented water in the wooden *furo* felt the same as it did at home. Like heated silk sliding across her skin. The hands scrubbing at Mariko's arms and shoulders did so in much the same way they'd done at home—without mercy, until her pale skin shone like that of a newborn child, pink and raw and perfect. A servant with permanent lines of judgment marring her brow yanked a comb inlaid with mother-of-pearl through Mariko's hair in much the same way her nursemaid had when she was younger.

It all felt so similar.

But if Mariko could be certain of nothing else now, she could be certain her life would never be the same again.

Under her brother's watchful care, they'd arrived to Inako late last night. To an imperial city cloaked in mourning. To streets teeming with whispers. Today was the funeral of their emperor, who had died suddenly, beneath a veil of suspicion. Upon discovering his body, the empress' wailing was said to have been heard across all seven *maru*. Even beyond the castle's iron-and-gold-plated double gates. She'd screamed murder. Raged at all those nearby, accusing them of treachery. It had taken a flock of maidservants to soothe her and begin ushering her toward her tears.

Toward final whimpers of resignation.

But beneath this hushed intensity seethed something sinister. Last night—when the second pair of gates leading to the castle had creaked closed behind their convoy—the air around Mariko had stilled. The faint breeze blowing past the woven screen of her *norimono* had sighed a final sigh. An owl had blared across the firmament, its cry ringing off the stone walls.

As though in warning.

Here in Inako, Mariko would not be granted a moment's respite. Nor did she wish for one. She would not allow herself anything of the sort.

For deep in the bowels of the same castle, the last in a line of celebrated shogun awaited his impending doom: the final judgment of the imperial city. And the lies this city wore— lies cloaked in silk and steel—shimmered beneath the surface, ready to take shape. No matter the cost, Mariko would mold them into what they should have been from the start:

The truth.

She bit down hard on nothing. Braced herself for the coming fight. It would be unlike any Okami and the Black Clan had taught her in Jukai forest. In this fight, she would not have weapons of wood and metal and smoke at her disposal. She would instead be armed with nothing more than her mind and her own mettle. This would be precisely the kind of fight she'd unknowingly prepared for as a child, when she'd pitted herself against her brother Kenshin.

In a game of wits against brawn.

Here in Inako, Mariko's armor would not be hardened leather and an ornamented helmet. It would be perfume and powdered skin. She had to convince Prince Raiden—her betrothed—to trust her. She needed him to cast her as the hapless victim instead of the willing villain.

Though I plan to be a villain in all ways.

If it took everything from Hattori Mariko—even her very life—she would not allow those she loved to fall prey to those set on destroying them. She would learn the truth about who conspired to kill her that day in the forest. Why they attempted to frame the Black Clan for the deed. And what deeper cause lay beneath their designs.

Even if those at the heart of the matter were the imperial family itself.

Even if her own family might fall into the crosshairs.

The thought sent a chill through her bones, as though the water in the *furo* had suddenly turned to ice.

It was clear Kenshin's choice had been made long before

he'd marched into Jukai forest flying their family crest alongside that of the emperor. Even before he'd let soldiers loose arrows around his only sister in a shower of fire and ash. But Mariko refused to align the Hattori name with that of the shiftless nobles in the imperial city. The same nobles intent on lining their pockets and gaining influence at the expense of the downtrodden. The same people they'd sworn to protect, like the elder woman who cared for the children in the Iwakura ward, who depended upon Okami and the Black Clan for support.

Protect.

Mariko drew her knees to her chest, shielding her heart, preventing the worst of her thoughts from taking root.

What if Okami is already dead?

She tightened the grip on her knees.

No. He isn't dead. He can't be. They will want to make a show of his death.

And I will be there to protect him when they do.

It was strange to think Mariko possessed the power to protect someone she loved. She'd never known the right words to do so before. Never known how to wield the right weapons. But ingenuity could be a weapon, in all its forms. Her mind could be a sword. Her voice could be an axe.

Her fury could ignite a fire.

Protect.

Mariko would never allow Okami—the boy who had stolen her heart in the dead of the night, deep within a forest of rustling trees—to lose all he had recently won. Nor would Mariko allow herself to lose anything she loved. She'd watched in the shadows as Kenshin had permitted soldiers to descend on her in Jukai forest. Felt the pang of her brother's betrayal with each of his questioning glances. She'd bit her tongue as these same soldiers had forced Okami to kneel in the mud and surrender. As they'd taunted and derided him from their lofty perches.

Mariko swallowed, the bitterness coating her throat.

Never again. I will protect you, no matter the cost.

"Look at your nails." The creases across the servant's brow deepened as she spoke, cutting through Mariko's musings. Her admonition conjured more memories of Mariko's childhood. "It's as though you've been digging through mud and stone all your life." She tsked, inspecting Mariko's fingers even further. "Are these the hands of a *lady* or a scullery maid?"

Her sight blurred as she gazed at her scarred knuckles. Another pair of hands took shape in her mind's eye, its calloused fingers intertwined with hers. Laced together. Stronger for it.

Okami.

Mariko blinked. Organized the chaos of her thoughts into something coherent. She bit her lip and widened her eyes. "The Black Clan . . . they made me work for them." Her voice sounded small. Insignificant. Exactly as she intended.

The servant chuffed in response, her expression still dubious. "It will take the work of an enchantress to repair this damage." Her words remained harsh, unmoved by the sight of Mariko's feigned timidity. Strangely—though this woman's rebuke was in no way comforting—it nevertheless warmed Mariko. It brought to mind her mother's quiet, ever-present judgment.

No. Not just that.

The servant reminded her of Yoshi.

At the thought of the grumblingly good-natured cook, Mariko's eyes began to water in earnest.

The servant watched her, an eyebrow peaking into her forehead.

That time, the sight of the older woman's judgment spurred a different reaction.

Anger roiled beneath Mariko's skin. She snatched her hand away and averted her gaze, as though she were afraid. Ashamed. The servant's stern expression lost some of its severity. As though Mariko's embarrassment was an emotion she could understand and accept. When she next took hold of Mariko's hand, her touch was careful. Almost soft.

In the same instant Mariko fought to curb her anger, she paused to take note.

My fear—even when it is feigned—has more weight when it is matched alongside anger.

One of the young women assisting the gruff servant bowed beside the wooden tub before lifting a pile of muddied, fraying clothing into the light. "My lady, may I dispose of these?" Her round face and button nose squinched in disgust.

They were the garments Mariko had worn in Jukai forest, when she'd been disguised as a boy. She'd refused to discard the faded grey *kosode* and trousers, even at Kenshin's behest.

They were all she had now. Her eyes widening in what she hoped to be a sorrowful expression, Mariko shook her head. "Please have them washed and stored nearby. Though I long more than anything to forget what happened to me, it is important to keep at least one reminder of the consequences when a wrong turn is taken in life."

The ill-tempered elder servant harrumphed at her words. Another young girl in attendance grasped one of Mariko's hands and began scrubbing beneath her nails with a brush fashioned from horsehair bristles. As she worked, the servant with the round face and button nose poured fine emollients and fresh flower petals across the surface of the steaming water. The colors of the oil shimmered around Mariko like fading rainbows. A petal caught on the inside of her knee. She dipped her leg beneath the water and watched the petal float away.

The image reminded her of what the old man at the watering hole had said the night she'd first met the Black Clan, disguised as a boy. He'd told her she had a great deal of water in her personality. Mariko had been quick to disagree with him. Water was far too fluid and changeable. Her mother had always said Mariko was like earth—stubborn and straightforward to a fault.

I need to be water now, more than ever.

Mariko wondered what had become of the Black Clan after Okami had surrendered to her betrothed. Wondered how Yoshi and Haruki and Ren and all the others had fared following such a dire blow. Only three nights past, they'd learned their leader had been deceiving them for years. He was not in fact the son of Takeda Shingen. The boy they'd followed and called "Ranmaru" for almost a decade was instead the son of Asano Naganori. He'd assumed the role of Takeda Ranmaru to protect his best friend and make amends for his father's betrayal—a betrayal that had resulted in the destruction of both their families. This boy's real name was Asano Tsuneoki.

They'd all been deceived.

And Mariko's betrothed—Prince Raiden—had left the forest with a prize worthy of laying at his father's burial mound.

The true son of Takeda Shingen, the last shogun of Wa: Okami.

Resentment smoldered hot and fast in Mariko's chest. Guilt coiled through her stomach. She dared to sit in a pool of scented water, allowing her skin and hair to be brushed and polished to perfection while so many of those she cared about suffered untold fates?

She took a steadying breath.

This was necessary. This was the reason she'd asked Kenshin to bring her to Inako. If Mariko intended to act on the plans she'd formulated while journeying from Jukai forest to the imperial city, she had to be in the seat of power. Mariko had to find a way to free Okami. She had to convince her betrothed that she was the willing, simpering young woman he surely desired in a bride. Then—once she'd earned a measure of trust—she could find a way to begin feeding information to the outside. To those who fought to change the ways of the imperial city and restore justice to its people.

To topple evil from its vaunted pedestal.

"Stand," the servant demanded in a curt tone.

Respect for an elder—regardless of status—drove Mariko to obey the truculent woman without question. She let the woman lead her to the largest piece of polished silver she'd ever seen in her life. Her eyes widened, and she stifled the urge to react to the sight of her naked body reflected back at her.

Her time in Jukai forest had changed Mariko on the outside as well. The angles of her face were more pronounced. She was thinner. What had been willowy before was now honed. Muscles she'd not known she'd possessed moved as she moved, like ripples across a pond.

She was stronger now, in more ways than one.

The elderly servant *tsk*ed again. "You're as thin as a reed. No young man will want to caress skin and bones, least of all one like Prince Raiden."

Again the urge to react rose in Mariko's throat. The truth blazed bright within her. She was more than an object of any man's desire. But on this particular score, the servant was right. She did need to eat if she intended to play the part.

Be water.

Mariko smiled through gritted teeth. Let her lips waver as though she were exhausted. Weak. "You're right. Please do whatever you can—whatever magic you possess—to restore me to my past self. To the sort of young woman who might please the prince. I want nothing more than to forget what happened to me." She struggled to stand taller. Fought to look proud.

Though the creases on her features deepened, the servant nodded. "My name is Shizuko. If you do as I say, it is possible we can remedy the effects of this . . . misfortune."

Mariko slid her arms into the proffered silken undergarment, wondering why the elder servant displayed such disdain for her. "Make me fit for a prince, Shizuko-*san*."

Shizuko sniffed and cleared her throat before directing the other servant girls to come forward. In their arms were more bolts of lustrous fabric. Piles of damask and painted silk, wrapped in sheets of translucent paper. Trays of jade and silver and tortoiseshell hairpieces.

Almost absentmindedly, Mariko ran the tip of a finger down the needled point of a silver hairpiece. Recalled one of the last times she had held one in her hand.

The night she'd pierced it through a man's eye for attacking her.

Mariko knew what she needed to do. For the sake of those she held dear, she needed to appear tall and proud.

And hapless.

She spoke in a near whisper, as though her words were nothing but an afterthought. "The imperial family will need me to appear strong, just as they are."

Just as they will need to be.

Because Hattori Mariko had a plan.

And this unwitting woman had already provided her with the first piece of the puzzle.

Novels by Renée Ahdieh

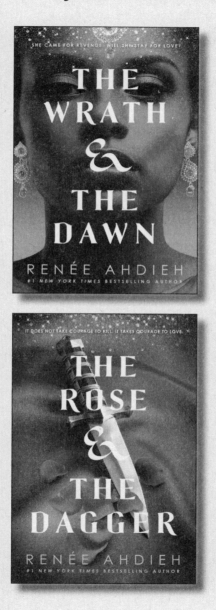